P9-DBL-846

Lasso the Moon

By Trish Holland
Illustrated by Valeria Petrone

To David and Jean Holland—
Thanks, Mom and Dad, for giving me the moon.
—T.H.

A GOLDEN BOOK • NEW YORK

Text copyright © 2005 by Trish Holland. Illustrations copyright © 2005 by Valeria Petrone. All rights reserved under International and Pan-American Copyright Conventions. Published in the United States by Golden Books, an imprint of Random House Children's Books, a division of Random House, Inc., New York, and simultaneously in Canada by Random House of Canada Limited, Toronto. Golden Books, A Golden Book, A Little Golden Book, the G colophon, and the distinctive gold spine are registered trademarks of Random House, Inc. Library of Congress Control Number: 2004106509
ISBN: 0-375-83289-0
MANUFACTURED IN THE UNITED STATES OF AMERICA
First Edition 2005
10 9 8 7

Time for bed, Little Tex.
Rio Rosie, good night.
Jump in your bunk beds
And close your eyes tight.

Now dream, little cowpokes.
Herd stars to the sky . . .

. . . Then make a wish
On the first star you spy.

A shooting star
Is galloping away.
Giddyup, little pardner,
And round up that stray!

Hitch up the chuck wagon
To a comet's tail,

So wranglers have vittles
On the star-dusty trail.

Now kindle some campfires
In the Milky Way,

So ranch hands can sing
"Yippee-ki-yi-ay!"

Lasso the moon.
Tug it way up high
As coyotes howl
A lullaby.

Mosey down a moonbeam.
The way home is clear.

"Git along, little dogies."
The barn is near.

Close the corral.
No more work to do
For a happy, sleepy
Buckaroo.

Cowboys and cowgirls,
Sweet dreams in the hay
Till you saddle the sun
And ride into the day.

goodnight